Under the Old Roof by Hesba Stretton

Hesba Stretton was the pen name of Sarah Smith who was born on July 27th 1832 in Wellington, Shropshire, the younger daughter of bookseller, Benjamin Smith and his wife, Anne Bakewell Smith, a devout Methodist. Although she and her elder sister attended the Old Hall school in town, they were largely self-educated.

Smith became one of the most popular Evangelical writers of the 19th century. She used her "Christian principles as a protest against specific social evils in her children's books." Her moral tales and semi-religious stories, mainly directed towards the young, were printed in huge numbers.

After her sister submitted, without her knowledge, a story on her behalf ('The Lucky Leg', was a bizarre tale of a widower who proposes to women with wooden legs) Smith became a regular contributor to Household Words and All the Year Round, two popular periodicals begun by Charles Dickens. Dickens would collaborate with many writers to produce his part-work stories. Smith writing under the pseudonym Hesba Stretton (created from the initials of herself and four surviving siblings: Hannah, Elizabeth, Sarah, Benjamin, Anna and the name of a Shropshire village; All Stretton) contributed a well-regarded short story, 'The Ghost in the Cloak-Room', as part of 'The Haunted House'. She would go on to write over 40 novels.

Her break out book was 'Jessica's First Prayer', published in the Sunday at Home journal in 1866 and the following year as a book. By the end of the century it had sold over one and a half million copies. To put that into context; ten times the sales of 'Alice in Wonderland'. The book gave rise to a strand of books about homeless children in Victorian society combining elements of the sensational novel and the religious tract bringing the image of the poor, under-privileged, child into the Victorian social conscious.

A sequel, 'Jessica's Mother', was published in Sunday at Home in 1866 and eventually as a book, some decades later, in 1904. It was translated into fifteen European and Asiatic languages as well as Braille, depicted on coloured slides for magic lantern segments of Bands of Hope programmes, and placed in all Russian schools by order of Tsar Alexander II.

Smith became the chief writer for the Religious Tract Society. Her experience of working with slum children in Manchester in the 1860s gave her books great atmosphere and, of course, a sense of authenticity.

In 1884, Smith was one of the co-founders, together with Lord Shaftesbury and others, of the London Society for the Prevention of Cruelty to Children, which then combined, five years later, with societies in other cities to form the National Society for the Prevention of Cruelty to Children. Smith resigned a decade later in protest at financial mismanagement.

In retirement in Richmond, Surrey, the Smith sisters ran a branch of the Popular Book Club for working-class readers.

Sarah Smith died on October 8th, 1911 at home at Ivycroft on Ham Common. She had survived her sister by eight months.

Index of Contents

UNDER THE OLD ROOF

Chapter I

Watling Street

Up in London, in the very heart of the City, there is a short and narrow street, with warehouses on each side so high as to keep the sunshine from the crowded pavement, along which heavy waggons, laden with goods, are passing to and fro all the day long. It is called Watling Street, and is part of the great Roman highway, running through the country from Kent to the far shores of Cardigan Bay. Here and there, in the heart of the country, as well as in the heart of the City, there are still to be found fragments of this grand old road. But Watling Street in the country is sure to be a lane, running between fields, yet so strongly and solidly made, that more than a thousand years of neglect, and of winter snows and summer tempests, have not materially injured it.

Over a hundred and fifty miles from London, there lies a mile or two of the old Watling Street between high hedgerows, making it almost as shady as the tall buildings which hang over it in London. The trees meet overhead, interlacing their leafy branches in the summer sunshine, or their delicate tracery of bare twigs against the frosty skies of winter. Now, as during the past centuries, purple briony creeps over the thorn-bushes, and wild rose-briars shoot up their tall, strong stems, with sprays of pink roses blooming upon them. Violets and primroses, cowslips and fox-gloves come and go in their due season, year after year; and soft mosses lie like velvet on the rough bark of gnarled trees, grown grey with the storms of uncounted winters. So straight is the line of the old Roman road that you can look far down it as through a long tunnel, lit up with a cool green light, as far as your eye can reach. Brilliant dragon-flies flit across if, and the happy birds haunt it with brisk fluttering of wings. And if no sound of human voices is to be heard, timid rabbits play along the grass-grown roadway, and pert squirrels come down from the trees to search for nuts under the hazel-bushes.

About a stone's throw from this fragment of Watling Street there stand three cottages, built half of timber, with high-pitched roofs of thatch, and gable windows rising out of the roof. They lie somewhat in a hollow, well guarded from keen winds, with a little brook, clear as crystal, running past them. Before and behind them there are old-fashioned gardens, well stocked with fruit-trees; and under the window of the largest of the cottages there stands a bench holding three beehives, from which a busy and joyous hum of happy labour issues from early dawn till late dusk. "Old Thorneycroft's houses in Watling Street" they are called by all the country round.

Old Thorneycroft's houses they had been; but by some stress of misfortune, the old builder had been compelled to sell them, having, however, secured a purchaser who engaged not to disturb him during his lifetime, and to give him the chance of rebuying his cottages for the same sum as that he had sold them for. For the rest of his life old Thorneycroft and his daughter Abigail had lived like misers, and worked like slaves: and when her father lay dying, Abigail promised him solemnly that she would give herself no rest until the place was her own again. He left her sixty pounds towards the two hundred that were needed; the fruit of his hardest toil, and his constant self-denial.

It was a few years after her father's death that Abigail married Richard Medlicott. For a long while her promise to her father weighed heavily against the thought of marriage. But Richard Medlicott had a pension of sixpence a day as a disabled soldier, and was a gifted man at shoemaking and cobbling. He had one child by a former marriage, a boy of ten, almost ready to get his own living, and Abigail at last consented to become his wife. Yet though he did not hinder her, he could not help her much towards attaining her end. She had to toil and strive, as it were, single-handed. The sun seldom rose before she did; and the moon and silent stars often shone down upon her as she dragged her weary limbs homewards, after a hard day's work in the fields or the farmhouses. Fortunately she had but one child; and her husband, who necessarily worked at home, took charge of him, after the first months of his infancy.

The harvest was over, and there was that gentle lull in country labour, which comes after the corn is gathered in, and the fields lie fallow, and the fruit is all ripened and plucked, and the hot hurry and burden of summer toil is ended. Once a week, when their work allowed of it, a few labourers from the scattered farmsteads round were accustomed to meet at Richard Medlicott's cottage, to hold what they still called their Society meeting. Like their founder, John Wesley, they had not forsaken the Church, but mostly attended the services there with sober regularity; but on Sunday evening, and once during the week, they held their own simple and homely worship in Richard Medlicott's kitchen, or in a little parlour which Abigail's father had built at the side of it. They had met together again on a Wednesday evening, after a dispersion of a few weeks, and dropped in, one by one, taking their customary seats in solemn silence, with just a word to one another until the worship of the evening was over.

It was a company of rugged, weather-beaten men and women, assembled in a bare little room which contained a wooden chair apiece, and a small three-legged table, on which lay the hymn-book, and the class-book in which their names were written. Abigail was a woman of sixty now, with grey hair and bowed shoulders; but she sat in her own corner to-night, with her hard brown hands lying restfully on her lap, as if their hardest toil was over. The spotless muslin border of her cap set off the deep russet and red of her sunburnt face, on which a smile of tranquil triumph was playing. Beside her on a low stool sat a tall, loose-limbed lad of twenty, her only child, poor Gideon, with the vacant eyes of a half-witted person, such as the country folk around call an innocent or natural, carefully avoiding the harsher name of idiot or fool. Gideon had sat there beside his mother, on the same low stool, ever since he was too old to go to bed before the class began; and though his name was not in the class-book, it was always called out by his father at the end of the others.

Old Richard put on his spectacles, and opened the hymn-book, and in a quavering yet measured voice gave out a familiar hymn:—

"No foot of land do I possess,
No cottage in the wilderness,

A poor wayfaring man."

But before the little company could pitch the right key for the well-known tune, Abigail broke in with eager yet tremulous tones:—

"No, Richard, no," she said; "I canna sing that hymn; niver again. The Lord, He's given me these cottages, and nigh on three acres o' land; and I canna sing those words in His face, not now. It runs in my head as I must praise Him in other words; but not those, Richard, niver again."

There was a thrill of excitement in the hearts of all the little company. Every one in the neighbourhood knew of Abigail's promise to her father, long since dead, and the steadfast way in which she had sought to keep it. It had seemed so great a task, that very few believed she could succeed; but what did her words mean, if she had not bought back the houses her father had sold?

"The rest on us can sing the old hymn, Aby," said her husband, with a quiet smile; "and there's words coming as thee can join in."

It was the custom among them to turn their faces to the wall as they sang; so that no one saw the tears of joy streaming down Abigail's wrinkled cheeks as she stood silently listening to words she could never sing again. But in a minute or two her voice, sweet still though thin and feeble, could join in with theirs.

"There is my house and portion fair,
My treasure and my heart are there,
And my abiding home.
For me my elder brethren stay,
And angels beckon me away,
And Jesus bids me come."

There seemed a new depth of meaning in these words to Abigail; her heart had been set on reclaiming her father's property, and the old house in which she had herself been born. But now her treasure and her heart must be in heaven. When her turn came to speak, she forgot the usual form of speech which for many years she had uttered with little variation. Her husband asked her as usual what the Lord's dealings with her had been since they last met in class, and she answered eagerly:—

"I don't know how to bless Him," she said; "He's given me my heart's desire. It's not my abidin' home, I know; but it was father's own house, and I shall die under my own roof; and Gideon, my boy, he's provided for; and if he dies, the old place'll go to thy son Dick, as thee loves so much, in spite of all. I canna bless the Lord enough."

Gideon had been listening to his mother with a perplexed and troubled face, missing the familiar form of speech which he had heard from time out of mind. When she came to an end with a sob, he broke in, his voice closely imitating hers:—

"I'm a poor sinner," he said; "but the Lord is my Saviour. I'm not fit to do more than the poor publican as stood afar off and smote his breast, and cried, 'God be merciful to me a sinner.' But, please God, I'll go on doin' my duty, and I hope nobody'll be turned away from Jesus by any sin o' mine. Amen."

They were the words he had heard his mother say, week after week, which he had always faithfully repeated in tones like her own. Abigail and Gideon were the last to speak; and now old Richard Medlicott gave out another hymn, prayed for a minute or two, and the meeting was over. They were free to gather about Abigail and wish her joy, and hear all the circumstances of her important purchase. The houses were her own at last. Although the money was hers in every sense, yet, being a married woman, the freehold was conveyed to her husband.

"Let us go out and look at 'em," said old Richard Medlicott.

Chapter II

Her Heart's Desire

Twilight was still lingering in the west, and the moon had risen; there was light enough to see the three cottages, with their high-pitched roofs standing clearly against the evening sky. The ruddy glimmers of the fires burning on the hearths shone through the lower casements, and the pale-grey wood-smoke rose slowly, and melted softly into the tranquil evening air. The little crowd of hard-working men stood at the end of the garden, looking back upon them with keener and more earnest eyes than usual. To buy them back was a great thing for a woman to have done.

"It's a pretty place," said Richard Medlicott; "'the blessing o' the Lord, it maketh rich, and He addeth no sorrow with it.' But, Aby, thee and me, we must remember as 'the time is short, and them that buy must be as though they possessed not.'"

"Ay," answered Aby; "I must think often on them blessed words, 'riches have wings, and they are soon cut off and we flee away.' I must na' glory in the houses, like proud Nebuchadnezzar, when he said, 'Isn't this great Babylon, that I've built with my own hand?' And he was driven out and dwelt among the beasts of the field, till his nails became like birds' claws. No, no; he's a warnin'! But it's the blessing o' the Lord that's made me rich; it isn't all my own hand."

It was plain to Abigail that her neighbours listened to her with more attention and respect than usual. Formerly they had not been so silent, or so ready to let her finish her speech without interruption. They called her Mrs. Medlicott, too; she, who until now had been plain Abigail, or even Aby. There was something inexpressibly sweet in this new deference shown to her, "We shan't see you in the fields again," said a waggoner from the nearest farm; "you'd do nought but house-work, now, I reckon, Mrs. Medlicott. Iverybody'll miss you, harvest-time, and weedin' and toppin' and tailin' turnips. It passes me where master'll get another to work as you've worked. But there's a end to all things, and you've no need to slave like a man no more."

"No," answered Abigail, trying to straighten her bowed shoulders, and to lift up her bent head, "I'm goin' to rest now, please God. I shall have more time to read my Bible and good books, like my husband. It seems as if I were goin' to have a week o' Sundays, like they've got in heaven above. A week o'

Sundays, with only little fid-fads to do; and the sun a-shinin', and the birds singin', and iverybody, all over the world, happy and good; that's what I think heaven's like, and it runs in my head as that's what my life's goin' to be, now my work's done."

They had sauntered down to the garden-wicket, arid after shaking hands with each of their departing friends, Richard and Abigail Medlicott slowly paced back along the moss-grown path, Gideon shambling behind them with dragging feet. He was talking to himself with a voice wonderfully like his mother's.

"I'm goin' to rest now, please God," he said; "and have a week o' Sundays, and think on the blessed words, 'Riches has wings, for they're soon cut off, and we flee away,' and Nebuchadnezzar, and proud Babylon that was driven out, and lived among the beasts. Poor Nebuchadnezzar!" he went on in his own natural tone; "I've hunted and hunted for him, scores o' times, among the beasts in the field all round, and I could never catch sight of him, poor old man, nor Babylon neither! But now my work's done, I'll have more time for seekin' him, shan't I, mother? It's time we had a week o' Sundays."

"God bless this house, and all that ever dwell under its old roof!" said Richard Medlicott, baring his white head as he crossed the door-sill. He had not been able to do much towards buying back the houses, except by cheerfully setting his wife free from many a household duty. It had fallen to his lot to be the one to stay at home, and watch patiently for the hour when the labourer's day was done, and his wife could return, worn out and weary, to the evening meal prepared for her by himself and Gideon. The careful thrift and constant self-denial, ordinarily the woman's part, had been practised by him, sometimes a little against the grain, but usually with a tranquil contentment that had made Abigail's task more easy. But he was thankful it was over.

He was growing old, over seventy years of age; and he could not look after Gideon as he used to do. It would make his last days more peaceful to have his wife oftener about the house.

It was well for him that Abigail had finished her task, for his strength began to fail fast that autumn. It is possible that it had begun to fail long before, unconsciously to his placid and contented nature. But now Aby was at home, moving to and fro with her brisk step, old Richard sat still in the warm chimney-corner, and began to feel how old he was. His well-worn Bible was more than ever in his hands, and now and then a prayer uttered half aloud would catch Abigail's ear.

"Lord, dear Lord!" he would say; "Thou'st given Aby her heart's desire; oh, give me mine. Didst Thou not hang on the accursed cross for us all? For my poor son Dick, as well as for every soul of man? He's a poor prodigal, Lord, that has sinned against Thee and me; but I forgive him, and wilt not Thou forgive him, Lord? Be it far from Thee to shut him out from Thy mercy. Oh, my son, my son! Would to God I could die for thee, my son, my son!"

It was some years since Abigail had uttered the name of her step-son, Dick Medlicott. She had striven hard to be a good mother to him, but he had always shown towards her a defiant and headstrong temper. His father had been weakly indulgent to him; and it had been impossible for her, not being the lad's mother, to set his father's mistakes right. She had borne with him and forgiven him until her patience was exhausted. And beneath the more open provocations there rankled in her mind the conviction, that it was through almost wilful carelessness of his that her boy, Gideon, had suffered the fall, which had caused his incapacity and helplessness. She was glad at heart when he disappeared, not only from home, but from the neighbourhood.

"Richard," she said to her husband, as Christmas drew near; "let's write a letter to Dick, and ask him to come and see thee once again. I'm ready to welcome him, for thy sake, if he'll come. But if he drinks, and curses, and storms, like he used to do, he'd be neither joy nor comfort to thee, I reckon."

"We dunna' know where the lad is," he answered.

"No; but Jenkins o' the 'Barley Mow,' he knows," she went on; "and he'd send the letter, if he wouldn't tell us where Dick is."

"I'll write and ask him, Aby," said the old man gladly; "but I'll let him know as there mustn't be any drinkin' or swearin' in the house now, no more than when he was a young lad. Thee'st forgiven him, Aby?" he added, in an anxious tone.

"Has he ever asked me to forgive him?" she replied; "our Lord tells us as they must turn and repent before we are to forgive 'em. The angels don't rejoice over a sinner till he's repentin'. Let him come home sorry for his sins, and I'll rejoice over him, and make much of him, for thy sake, Richard. But I couldn't bear him to come teachin' my Gideon to curse and drink; that 'ud break my heart, God knows."

"Ay! and mine," he answered.

It was a long letter old Richard Medlicott wrote to his prodigal son, earnestly entreating to see his face once more before he died. But though the letter was sent to him, they received no answer, except through Jenkins of the "Barley Mow," who repeated Dick's short message with an oath, that he would never set foot again in a house where a woman was the master.

Chapter III

Abigail's Promise

Very probably poor Abigail had been masterful in the house. It had been her father's dwelling, and the place where she was horn. When she married, instead of going to her husband's house, he had come to hers. He had not long been discharged from the army on his small pension, and the possessions he had brought with him were very trifling; whilst all the simple and homely furniture of the house had belonged to Abigail. She had done the man's work, too, toiling abroad, or digging in their little patch of ground, as a man would do. To stand by patiently and see Dick growing up idle and rebellious had been impossible to her. And now that the place, with the two adjoining cottages, was her own, bought back by her own and her father's earnings, she did not feel less masterful. All the neighbours treated her as a woman of more importance than while she was merely a labourer in the fields, or a charwoman in the farm-houses; and Abigail enjoyed the difference.

But as the winter chill passed into the biting winds of March, it was known that old Richard Medlicott was dying. Abigail could hardly believe it. She had been so busy all these years that she had had no time to think how likely it was that she would lose her husband, who was nearly fifteen years older than herself. She had hardly noticed how infirm he was growing; and the old man, never given to murmuring, had scarcely been conscious of it himself. Gradually he had left oft doing little things that were beyond his strength, and set Gideon to do them under his oversight; but both he and Abigail had fancied it was in order to keep the restless lad occupied. Like all other old men, Richard Medlicott would have been reluctant to confess that he could no longer do what he had once been in the habit of doing easily.

The room under the thatched roof where he lay dying was the same room where Abigail had seen her father and her mother die. All the sacred memories of her life were gathered there. Her husband's white head rested on the pillow where her father's had lain before; and his dim eyes looked out through the same low easement upon the same garden and fields beyond. She, too, was sitting on the same seat, patiently, yet with tears, waiting for the same parting.

"Aby," he said; "'there is a time to be born, and a time to die,' and behold! my time to die is nigh at hand. The Master is callin' me to be where he is. But thou'lt miss me, Aby?"

"Ay!" she answered, weeping; "I'd sooner ha' missed buyin' back the houses than ha' lost thee, Richard. It'll be a time to weep wi' me, if God's goin' to take thee from me."

"Nay, but thou'lt find a refuge under the shadow o' his wings," he said; "think o' that, Aby. The shadow o' His wing! That's a surer shelter than thy own roof. I can leave thee and Gideon under the covert o' God's wings; but would to God my poor Dick was there! Only he will not hide himself from the misery that is comin' upon him; the misery o' the wrath of God."

The old man turned away his sunken and withered face towards the wall, as if even his wife could not share the anguish of his soul over the prodigal son, who was not her child as well as his own. Abigail knelt down beside the bed, and stretched her brown sinewy arm across him.

"Dick shall always find a home here," she said, with a sob; "the same as if I was his own mother. I'll forgive him, and bear with him; ay! I forgive him now, afore he asks my pardon, for thy sake, Richard. Don't thou fret so over him. The Lord's patience is more than mine, and can never be worn out. Thou'lt bid him welcome to heaven some day; for thou'lt niver be heart-happy wi'out him, God knows. Let us pray he may come right at last, Richard. Nothing's too hard for the Lord."

She spoke with quick, short sobs; and for a few minutes there was silence, whilst the old man pressed her arm against him with his feeble hands. Through all the years they had lived together, Dick had been the only root of bitterness in their hearts. But now he was going away, was about to die without seeing his son's face again, and Aby was ready to promise anything that could lighten the burden of his great sorrow. Let Dick come when he would, he should be dear to her for his father's sake.

"Richard," she said at last, after a long pause; "dost think as God Almighty has less patience, and loves Dick less than me?"

"No, no," he replied; "that's impossible with the Lord."

"And if I promise thee to keep a home open for him," she went on, in a trembling voice, "won't God Almighty, and Him as died to save him, keep heaven open for him? Some day, when thou'rt lookin' over the jasper walls o' heaven, thou'lt see him comin', a long way off, nearer and nearer, till the pearly gates open for him, and thou'lt fall on his neck and kiss him. Don't reckon the Lord harder than me; and I'll niver shut my door against thy son Dick."

Her heart was very full as she uttered her promise. A swift vision passed before her of Dick coming back a penitent, worn out and weary with his own sins, and ready to accept the quiet home she could give to him. What a comfort he might be to her, even yet! He, a man over thirty, whilst she was growing old, and in a few years must come to her own hour of death, Who could she leave Gideon to so well as to his own brother, if that brother was a converted man? Oh! if the Lord would but bring Dick back as one of those repentant sinners, over whom there is joy in the presence of the angels of God!

It was growing dark, though the moon had risen, and shone through the lattice window upon her husband's white head. But she did not care to stir. There was a quiet rustling of ivy under the eaves, where the swallows' nests were waiting for the return of their wanderers. In the garden below, the fruit-trees were quickening, and pushing out their first leaf-buds; and the daisies in the little croft beyond had opened many days ago. Only to-day she had heard a low, mysterious hum in the beehives under the window; the bees would be awake as soon as the flowers were blooming. Spring was coming again, as it had come to her for sixty years in this old home; it was close at hand, but never had her heart felt so heavy in the spring-time.

"Shall I light a candle for thee, Richard?" she asked.

"No," he answered, feebly; "there's no more sun nor moon for me, Aby. 'The Lord shall be unto me an everlastin' light, and my God my glory.' And thine, too, and Gideon's, Aby."

"Ay!" she sobbed.

"It's dark," he said; "but there's glory beyond. 'The Lord shall be thine everlastin' light, and the days o' thy mournin' shall be ended;' the days o' thy mournin', my poor Aby. They'll all come to an end. When thou'rt a widow woman, in darkness and desolation, look to Him that is thine everlastin' light."

"Ay, I will!" she sobbed again.

She sat still for a long while in the moonlit room, with her hard hands folded on her lap, and her eyes fastened on the dim features of her husband's beloved face. So quiet it was, that she could hear the ticking of the clock in the kitchen below, and the hissing of the faggots burning on the hearth, and the merry chirping of the cricket that was basking in the warmth. Gideon had been away all day, for now and then he would wander for miles around, coming home foot-sore and weary, but radiant with untold delight; and Abigail had long since ceased to fear any harm happening to him. But to-night, when his father was dying, there was something sad and lonesome in his absence; and she wished Gideon was beside her, though he could not understand what was about to happen.

"Behold!" said the slow, faint, measured voice of the old man, in solemn yet glad surprise; "'His countenance is as the sun shining in his strength!'"

He had lifted himself up on his low bed, and was stretching out his withered feeble hands, as though he saw one ready to grasp them. His voice was stronger and clearer as he spoke again.

"And He laid his right hand upon me, saying unto me, 'Fear not; I am the first and the last; I am He that liveth, and was dead; and behold I am alive for evermore!'"

There was strange triumph and gladness in his tones; and Abigail, who was standing by earnestly gazing at him, was almost afraid to draw near to him. And before she could reach him, and throw her arms about him, he had sunk back again on the bed.

"Amen, even so, come, Lord Jesus!" he sighed in a breathless whisper. The old white head fell back, and his outstretched hands dropped. For a few minutes Abigail felt his heart beat feebly under her hand, and then all was over. Another life was ended under the old roof.

Chapter IV

Is it Just?

In the secret depths of her heart Abigail felt stricken and desolate; but she had never been so dependent upon her husband as most women are, and it was no part of her nature to make a great display of her feelings. Her husband's death brought but little change to her circumstances. There was no necessity to be looking out for another and a poorer dwelling-place, as if she had been the widow of some farm-labourer, whose cottage would be needed for his successor. There were no money troubles to face. Her house was her own, and the two adjoining cottages brought in four shillings a week. She could take in a lodger who would pay two shillings a week more; and there was her garden produce, and the honey and wax from the hives, which alone had never failed to bring in from three to four pounds a year. She was a widow, well on in years, and almost past work; but she was well off, and there was no reason to dread the future, either for herself or Gideon.

Gideon missed his father, as a faithful dog might have missed him, pining somewhat, and diligently seeking him about his old haunts. Abigail had not allowed him to attend the funeral, or even see his father's dead body, knowing that she could never make him understand what death is. She could not bring herself to let him see all that seemed his father nailed down in a coffin, and buried in the churchyard.

"I've searched for father everywhere," Gideon would say, wistfully; "and sometimes I catch a sight of him a long way off, in among the woods, or up the hills, wi' his white hair all shining in the sun, and when I reach the place, he's gone."

"His master Jesus Christ has sent for him," she answered again and again; "and thou and me, we'll niver see his face no more, till we are fit to go to the place where he is. Thee canna find him if thou search all thy life long. He's gone to live with the Lord Jesus."

"But if father's livin', and the Lord Jesus is livin', why canna I find 'em and see 'em?" he asked, with the rare tears in his bright and wandering eyes.

"We canna look at the sun," she said; "it's over bright for our eyes. And they're too bright for us to see 'em with our common eyes, Gideon. When we are fit to see them, then our eyes'll be strong enough; but niver, niver till then."

Yet still Gideon, with his short memory and his unsettled fancies, continued to search for his lost father. She could hear him calling "father" over the garden hedge, where Richard had long ago made a rude seat, under a walnut-tree, and had been often used to rest there. Sometimes he would come in hurriedly, and take down his father's old hat and coat, which still hung in their places behind the door, and turn them over with a pensive sadness on his usually happy face. And when Sunday came he would sit with his father's old Bible before him, poring over the yellow leaves, as if they would tell him the secret of his father's absence, and how long it would be before he would come home again.

Why! here's a letter from father! he cried joyfully one Sunday afternoon, about a month after old Richard Medlicott's death. It was a half-sheet of paper, written with a shaking and feeble hand, and laid between the leaves of the book he had read most often. Abigail took it into her own hands with some awe; a paper written by her dear husband was a matter of solemn importance to her.

"This is Richard Medlicott's Last Will, being of sound mind, thank God Almighty for it! I give to my son Richard Medlicott all my goods that I possess, except my old Bible which I leave to my dear wife Abigail Medlicott. It is no good leaving anything to my poor Gideon. But Dick is to have my watch, and my medals, and the little keepsakes as belonged to his mother. I leave everything to him, save the old Bible, with my love to Abigail, my faithful wife. And may God have mercy on Dick's soul! Amen."

The paper was signed by two of the friends, who were accustomed to come to the Society meeting every Wednesday. Poor Abigail read it with a feeling of loving awe. She had never thought of her husband making a will; wills were seldom thought of by people of their class. When a man died he usually left so little behind him, that what there was, was divided without the formality of a will. Nor had Richard Medlicott much to dispose of; yet he had considered it his duty to bequeath that little to his eldest son, rebel and prodigal as he was. The watch, and the medals, and the little keepsakes, were all safe; and Dick should have them as soon as he pleased.

It was Sunday evening; Easter Sunday, which fell late that year. There was to be no service in the cottage, for the rural dean was preaching at church, and every one was gone to hear him. Abigail had been twice to church that day, and visited the new grave there; but Gideon had been rambling along the old Roman road for miles, and was tired now, willing enough to keep house while his mother went down to the village.

Abigail, in her widow's cap and dress, sauntered tranquilly along the lanes, and over the fields, as familiar to her as the lines of a beloved mother's face. She had never been more than ten miles away; and she had weeded and harvested with her own hands in most of the fields she crossed. The world was not large and wide to her; it was a little circle filled with people well known to her, and with but few changes visiting it. As she went along, her eyes fell on the young thistles springing up, where they sprang up last year and many years before, among the shooting corn. The lambs playing about the meadows might have been those that were playing there fifty years ago, when she was a child, so exactly were they like those of that olden time. The timid field-mice scuttled away from before her approaching feet, as they had done when she walked with the swift steps of a girl. The old church-spire among the dark yew-trees in the quiet churchyard surrounding it, had been the first symbol pointing her heaven-wards; and the sound of its bells, ringing as they were now, had been the earliest and sweetest music that had fallen upon her ear.

It was dusk when the reached the village-inn, and the lights shone through its uncurtained windows. She was come to tell Jenkins of the "Barley Mow," about her husband's will, and to ask him to let Dick know of it. Yes; Jenkins was at home this Sunday evening, quietly sitting in his bar-parlour beside a table, with a jug, and two bright pewter tankards upon it. And opposite to him—was it possible her old eyes, growing a little dim after sixty years' hard work, could deceive her? Was it possible that yonder dark, scampish, dissipated looking man, with pampered face, and bleared red eyes, could be her dead husband's son, her own stepson, Dick Medlicott?

Abigail felt as if her heart had been suddenly seized with a hot hand, and held in a tight grip. She could not move her feet to take a step forward, but stood staring in through the window, as if she had been turned to stone. Dick looked worse, far worse than when he left home, and went away to London. Worse! yes, by ten years of idle self-indulgence and wilful wrong-doing. This was no repentant prodigal, though his clothes were all rags, and the shoes on his outstretched feet were worn into great holes, through which his bare and dusty skin was plainly seen. His whole aspect was that of an unreclaimed and hardened vagabond. Yet this was her dear husband's son, for whom she had promised solemnly to have her door always open to him, and to make him welcome to her home and Gideon's!

She did not know how long she stood there shivering, but not with cold. The two men were in earnest conversation, but they spoke so low that she could not even catch the sound of their voices. At last she gathered courage and strength enough to go on, and stood just within the doorway of the close and offensive room.

"Is that you, Dick?" she asked, in a faltering voice.

Both Jenkins and Dick started, and stared at her with wide-open eyes; Abigail had never crossed that threshold before, since Jenkins had been landlord of the "Barley Mow," and it had lost its old name for respectability.

"Why! we were a-talking of you," exclaimed Jenkins, with a rough laugh; "talk of what's-his-name, you know, and you'll see his horns! Dick here was telling me what's brought him all the way from London."

"He knew his father was dead!" said Abigail, looking steadfastly at her slovenly and degraded stepson.

"I knew that there weeks ago," he answered with a sneer; "trust me for coming over only for that!"

"He was a good father, Dick," she said gently; "and he prayed for you as he lay a-dying, and fretted over you very sore. Ay! and to comfort him all I could I promised him faithful to keep my home always open to you, come home whenever you would. And I'm bound to keep to my word. There's a bed, and a supper ready for you to-night if you'll come home wi' me. And there's all your father's clothes, and his watch, and his medals, and his keepsakes as were your mother's; they are all for you. Your father left 'em all to you."

There was an odd look on the faces of both of the men as they listened to her, which frightened Abigail. Jenkins wore a smile of triumph; whilst Dick seemed as if he was carrying off an uneasy sense of shame, under an expression of fierce determination.

"Your house!" he said, slowly; "why! it's mine."

So outrageous sounded such a declaration in Abigail's ear that she laughed, though not a woman much given to laughing. But the trembling that had come over her when she first caught sight of Dick did not cease; she shook more and more, and not to betray it, she was forced to sink down on the chair nearest to her.

"Ay! it's mine," asserted Dick; "houses and lands go to the eldest son, when the father dies."

"But they never were thy father's," answered Abigail; "all the folks round know as they once belonged to my father, and that I bought 'em back again. There's no secret about it; everybody knows as the houses are mine."

"And I say they're mine," reiterated Dick, bringing his clenched fist heavily down on the table; "a married woman's goods go to her husband, whether it's houses, or lands, or money, if there's not any settlin' of 'em on herself, afore she's married. Father never settled the houses on you, to be yourn, did he? And he never made a will, and left 'em to you, did he?"

"He hadn't nothin' to leave but his watch, and his medals, and his keepsakes," answered Abigail, in a high-pitched tone of excitement; "but he made a will, and I only found it this evenin', in his old Bible. I came along to ask Jenkins to let you know; but you'll see as he hadn't nothin' else to leave to ye."

The faces of both the men fell as they heard of the will, and Dick snatched it eagerly out of her trembling hand. But he shouted a loud shout of triumph as he read the words, "I give to my son Richard Medlicott all my goods that I possess, except my old Bible."

"Why! it makes me doubly sure!" he cried; "all that you had was his, and he leaves me all save his old Bible, and you're kindly welcome to that."

"Ay, ay!" said Jenkins; "I know the law, and by the law a married woman is nobody, and she can't hold houses, or lands, or money, without a special lawyer's dokiment about it. If you've got a lawyer's dokiment, Mrs. Medlicott, you've only got to show it. What a woman earns isn't her own, if she doesn't get a magistrate's protection for it, or how should I get all the money owing me, I should like to know? You never got a magistrate's protection for your earnings, did you? So the houses and the money was your husband's. And he's left all he had to Dick; and if he hadn't made his will, houses and lands go to the eldest son, all over England. That's the law, and all the lawyers and the judges'll tell you the same. So Dick's come down to take possession of his father's goods."

But Abigail scarcely heard the last few words. The room seemed whirling round her, and her heart was beating heavily, heavily. She could hear and see nothing distinctly; but in her inmost soul there seemed to be a still, low whisper saying, "I will trust in the covert of Thy wings!" But for this she must have fallen, heart-broken, to the ground. It was some minutes before she regained sight and hearing, though there was a hazy vision of the two men before her eyes, and a confused murmur of their voices in her ears. As soon as she could lift herself up she crawled to the door, and made haste to leave the hateful house.

Chapter V

The Workhouse Roof

The fresh keen air of the quiet night helped to bring Abigail to the full use of her senses, and by-and-by the nervous trembling of her limbs almost ceased. Still she felt stunned and bewildered, and her footsteps were slower, and less firm than usual. As she wended her way slowly homewards she tried vainly to remember and realise all Jenkins and Dick had been saying to her. Though the Easter moon was at the full, the sky was overcast, and only now and then the soft, silvery light fell upon her path. But to Aby the road home from the village was as well known and as safe as the floor of its father's house to the smallest child; there was no old tree-root, stretching itself across the narrow pathway to trip up unwary feet, that she did not know. Yet even on this familiar tract she felt her steps falter in the darkness, and it was late before she reached home.

But when she found herself at the old garden-gate, and the thatched roofs of her father's cottages stretched in black outlines against the cloudy sky, and the fruit-trees her father had planted swayed a little in the low night-wind, and she could see the glimmering of the fire on the hearth where she had spent all her life, then the trembling came upon her again as violently as ever. She could hardy crawl down the long walk, bordered with flower-beds; and when, at length, she gained her own fire-side, she sank down in her old chair, and remained there unable to stir, until long after the fire had burned itself out into a heap of grey ashes. She could hear Gideon's regular breathing in the room overhead, where he was sleeping soundly like a little child. He would never be anything but a little child, no great, strong son, who would be able to stand up for her, and protect her. There was no one to help her, not one.

So far as her houses were in question that was true. The law of the land was against her. It would be all in vain to prove that they had belonged to her father, and had been bought back again by the careful earnings of his hands and her own. It could never have crossed her mind to seek protection for her earnings against the kind and gentle old man who had been her husband. There was no remedy for it: Dick must have all, and she and her own boy must turn out for him. There would be no refuge for them but the workhouse.

Yet Abigail could not believe it; she felt as if God Himself must interfere to hinder so terrible an injustice, and so bitter a calamity. The neighbours came to see her, and did not spare to cry out and clamour against Dick. Mrs. Merridew and her daughter, who lived as tenants in the next cottage, gave notice at once to leave it, when Abigail was turned out. All the country cried shame on him; but no signal judgment befell him. Poor Abigail could not pray for it, though in her secret heart she looked for it, and was sorely baffled and perplexed as the days passed by, bringing nearer and nearer the hour when she and Gideon would be turned ignominiously out of doors, vagrants, without a home on the face of the earth.

That hour, like all other inevitable hours, came at last. Jenkins was to receive the keys from her; and she watched him coming along the quiet Watling Street, where the hawthorne bushes were blossoming, now in sight, and now hidden by the trees, up to the old garden-gate, where she and Gideon were waiting. For now she was sure there was no redress, Abigail knew how to act with simple dignity and decision. The law was cruel and Dick was cruel; and the Lord had not sent her help in the hour of her sorest need. She had trusted in the covert of His wings, and behold! her own roof was taken away from her, and she stood there, a weary worn-out old woman, burdened with a helpless son. "Though He slay me, yet I will trust in Him," she said, with a half-broken heart.

She did her best to take up her old life of incessant toil; but she soon discovered that her former strength was gone. There was no longer the possibility of hard work in her. Her brown arms, with their strained and starting sinews, could no more be trusted to lift and carry heavy weights, and her eyes, once so bright and keen, seemed to have grown strangely dull and dim. Even her memory was not what it used to be. The small duties of her old home she could have managed easily enough for years to come; but it would never be in her power again to earn her own bread, anti Gideon's,

"Lord," she would say, not aloud, but in the silent depths of her aching heart; "I canna tell what Thee art after. Thee has taken away my husband, and given me a poor, soft innocent of a child, God bless him! and now Thee has let the prodigal son come home, anti turn his brother and me out o' door's. That isn't like Thy good. book, O Lord! But Thy will be done. Richard's with Thee somewhere, and can no more help me; or Thou'd surely stay Thy hand if he prayed Thee to leave me a-be. If Richard's content, I'll try to be content. I'm ready to go into the workhouse if it's Thy will; only it's hard to shut up my poor Gideon there, away from his old mother. He'll break his heart, Gideon will, shut up in them close walls. But if it's the Lord's will to break our hearts, Thy will be done!"

There was no workhouse near her old home; for in those thinly-peopled parishes it was necessary for several of them to join in making provision for paupers. The "Union," as the common workhouse was called, was situated in a small town some miles away, an utterly unknown place to Abigail. For a few things this circumstance would be some little alleviation of her distress. Her father had been a thrifty, industrious man, even ambitious in his own rank; and she had been a true daughter to him. But now, if she, his only child, and Gideon, his only grandchild, were to become the melancholy inmates of a workhouse, it would be better for no old neighbour's eye to see them in their pauper uniform.

But oh! the utter misery of being cut off altogether from all the old scenes and the old faces that till now had filled up for her the space and time which we call life? It was, in truth, harder and more bitter than death itself to Abigail. If she had been about to die there was Richard in that unknown land over the river, waiting to welcome her; and not only Richard, but her father, and many a friend who had crossed before her, with whom she had gone down, step by step, to the very brink of the chilly waters, until the path, so often trodden, had become familiar to her. She knew how to die, and had those who loved her on the far shore; but she did not know how to go into the workhouse, and she had not a single friend there.

But as the summer passed on, and the few shillings she could earn failed to keep her and Gideon in food, to say nothing of rent and clothing, Abigail knew that nothing else lay before them. At last one morning, bidding farewell to no one, and with nothing in her possession but her husband's old Bible, and a few articles of clothing belonging to herself and Gideon, she set oft on the long day's tramp, the end of which was the solitary refuge left to her.

"Where are we goin', mother?" asked Gideon.
"To another house, my lad," she answered.
"Is it my father's house?" he asked again.
"No," she said.
"Is it God's house?" he went on.

"No, no," she cried; "it's the workhouse. Yet, may be, it's God's house to us, if it's His will we are to live in it."

Chapter VI

It had been in fact a great surprise to Dick Medlicott to find the law altogether on his side in the unscrupulous act he had just committed. In London he had fallen in with a broken-down and drunken lawyer's clerk, who had put it into his head to assert his unjust and unjustifiable, yet legal claim to his step-mother's property. He knew very well that a word of warning to his father would have put matters right, by causing him to make a will, securing to his wife the fruits of her own and her father's labours. But no such friendly warning had reached Richard Medlicott or Abigail; and the law itself pronounced his title as eldest son absolute.

There was naturally a bitter feeling against him throughout all the countryside; and never was a man more completely sent to Coventry. Men who were not at all sensitive to high or fine feelings of honour turned their backs upon him; and Abigail's old friends and employers openly denounced him. Not a single soul, except Jenkins of the "Barley Mow," was friendly with him, and no workman would admit him as a companion in his work. More serious still, as it seemed to him, no tenant offered himself for the cottage left vacant by the dressmaker and her mother; and his other tenant, a man working on the railway, was looking out for another home, and he and his wife refused to exchange even a brief good-day with him. There was a general impression abroad that some very signal judgment would befall him, or the houses so unfairly conic by; and considering how regularly Dick went to bed drunk, leaving his fire and candle to burn themselves out, and how dry the half-timber walls and thatched roof were, there would have been nothing miraculous or marvellous in the fact, if the cottages had all been burnt down to the ground in a single night.

Under the influence of his friend the London lawyer, and of Jenkins of the "Barley Mow," Dick Medlicott had gone further than he intended to do in turning his step-mother and half-brother out of doors, and forcing them into the workhouse. His own half-formed notion dimly floating in his muddled brain, had been to make himself master of this house, and to keep them still at home in it, knowing what a thrifty, industrious housekeeper Abigail was, and how much work could be got out of Gideon by good management. He had never counted upon living absolutely alone in the old place, with no more frequented road than the Watling Street running past it, and a mile away from the "Barley Mow," with a homeward path from it not quite as safe as he could wish when he had had a drop too much. If Gideon had been at home he could have kept him waiting his pleasure to guide him safely along the rough field track, skirting deep ditches, where there was often water enough to drown a man; and over the unguarded foot-bridge, with not even a hand-rail to steady oneself by, under which the brown stream sometimes rushed with a swift and swirling current. As it was, he dared not get as drunk as he could wish: he could never go far enough to reach the point at which drunkenness was a pleasure to him. He cursed the out-of-way place, and the rough road every night; but no cursing tended to mend matters.

Besides all this, Dick found that after all the small income was a very trilling affair. Abigail, by her ceaseless thrift and management, would have made it enough for herself and Gideon to live happily on; but it did not go far towards the maintenance of a man, idle and self-indulgent as he was. He had lost one tenant, and the other was going. Oddly enough the bees were dying, the neighbours said because Abigail had forgotten to tell them there was a death in the house, and had not even bound a bit of crape on the hives. The summer was a wet one, and when the autumn came there was scarcely any fruit on the famous pear and. plum trees; and as he had neglected the garden in the spring-time there was but a poor store of vegetables for the winter. Dick had come down from London fancying he should be quite a gentleman with three cottages and two acres of land of his own, and his step-mother and Gideon to wait upon his pleasure. But how different was the reality!

It was a relief to him one day to see the postman, who rarely turned aside to Watling Street, come up the narrow garden walk with a letter in his hand. Dick was in low spirits that morning, as he usually was until noon had passed, and he found his way to the "Barley Mow." The postman spoke not a word, but delivered his letter into his hand and strode away again. He opened it and found it contained these lines written in a large and clear, though clumsy hand.

"Bread of deceit is sweet to a man, but afterwards his mouth shall be filled with gravel."

"Whoso curseth his father or his mother, his lamp shall be put out in obscure darkness."

"An inheritance may be gotten hastily at the beginning, but the end thereof shall not be blessed."

"He, that being often reproved, hardeneth his heart, shall soon be destroyed, and that without remedy."

The paper was signed by all the men and women who had been in the habit of meeting every Wednesday evening in Richard Medlicott's cottage. Dick read the verses and they haunted him. As he stumbled homewards alone through the dense darkness of the winter nights, he found himself repeating the words, "His lamp shall be put out in obscure darkness;" whilst often, as he sat at his solitary and meagre meals, for which he had no appetite, his conscience would whisper, "His mouth shall be filled with gravel." After the busy roar of London streets and the constant hustling among his fellow-men, who bore him no ill-will, this dread stillness of the country, haunted by threatenings like these, made his hastily-gotten inheritance hateful to him.

"If yo' ever think of parting with your houses and land," said Jenkins to him one day, "yo'll give me the first refusal of them?"

Jenkins had had his eye on Abigail's cottages for many a long year, never believing she would scrape together money enough to buy them back again. But now was his opportunity. Dick was deeply in his debt, having been made welcome to anything in the "Barley Mow," but seeing nothing of the long score chalked up against him on the back of the cellar door, and transferred to Jenkins' books every Sunday morning, whilst the house was closed during church time. Jenkins was in haste to get possession of the houses, for they were already showing signs of decay. The thatch of the unoccupied cottage was looking damp and mildewed, and the gardens were getting full of weeds, and the trees and hedges were untrimmed. Jenkins began to think he must push Dick on, or the place would lose half its value.

"I've a good mind to sell 'em," answered Dick, heavily, "and go back to London; there's some life there. But I'll ask lawyer Cornfield about the price afore sayin' anythin' to you. Yo're over sharp for me, yo' are, Jenkins."

Dick meant the last words as a compliment, but Jenkins had been drinking slowly all day, and was in an irritable and uncertain temper. He took them as an insult, especially as they were coupled with a reference to Dick's other friend, the London lawyer. He turned away with a sneer to the desk where his ledger lay, in a corner behind the settle.

"I'm alookin' what your score is, Dick Medlicott," he said; "and whenever you sell Watling Street houses, there'll be my score to pay. Lawyer's price here or lawyer's price there, yo'll have to pay me my score."

"I'll pay it now if you're hard up for money," answered Dick, carelessly; "how much is it?"

"Over forty pounds," said Jenkins, in a tone of sulky triumph.

Over forty pounds! Dick had never possessed five pounds at once in his life, and here was Jenkins telling him that when he sold his inheritance, over forty pounds must be paid out of the sum he would receive. He had often paid small sums for his liquor; and had but a dim idea that he might be in debt, as Jenkins had never mentioned it till now. As his brain, sobered by the shock, cleared a little, and he saw the trap into which he had let himself be caught, his anger rose. He flung the tankard that was in his hand at Jenkins, who was standing with the lid of the desk resting on his head.

"Yo're a swindlin' raskill!" he shouted.

Two or three minutes later Dick Medlicott found himself pitched and kicked into the village street, and the door of the public-house locked against him. He had left his coat inside, but presently it was flung out to him through the window. The night was very dark and cold, as he wrapped it well about him; and, swearing savagely at every step, he set his face homewards.

It was so dark that more than once he missed his footing, and fell heavily on the ground, lying there helplessly, until the sharp and bitter sting of the frost forced him to rise, and stumble on again. He knew that if he had been as drunk as usual, he would have been found by some passer-by next morning, a man frozen to death. For very dread of crossing the foot-bridge, beneath which the icy stream was flowing, not noisily but stealthily, with its half-frozen waters, he lingered till every limb was benumbed, and then he crept over it on all fours, with great drops of moisture starting out on his forehead, in spite of his numbness. "His lamp shall be put out in obscure darkness," he muttered half aloud. But he crawled across in safety, and reached home at last, too weary and too chilled to do anything but creep into bed, dressed as he was, and sleep off both his fatigue and drunkenness.

Chapter VII

Dreams and Visions

When Dick Medlicott awoke the next morning he felt at once feverish, yet chilled to the bone. His eyes fell on the torn and dirty coat he had wrapped around him, and saw that it was ten times more torn and dirty than his own; he recognised it as belonging to a tramp who had been drinking in the "Barley Mow." But he had not spirit enough to face Jenkins this morning. He dragged himself up, and lit a fire, longing in vain for a cup of warm tea to refresh his parched tongue. There was no tea in the house, and little else, besides a small loaf which he had bought in the village the day before. He sat shivering over the fire, with a head that ached intolerably, and felt as if a flame was burning in his brain, though his body trembled with cold. The day seemed as if it would never come to an end, but the night was worse still; the darkness made the long hours intolerable.

The next morning he crawled to his door, and shouted again and again to his tenant in the farther cottage. But their house-door opened at the other side, and it was a long while before he saw one of the children, and bade him go in and tell his mother that he was very ill. Presently the boy returned, and called to him over the garden hedge.

"Mother says as there's a deal o' small-pox about," he shouted, "and she daren't come anigh; but she'll send for the doctor, and bid him come."

Dick crept back to the old hearth, and sat down in his father's old arm-chair. If he had caught the small-pox, he said to himself, it was from wearing and sleeping in that dirty coat, which had been exchanged for his own at the "Barley Mow," maliciously, as he thought. Again the long hours paused wearily, as he sat up till midnight for the doctor, who never came. There was no sleep for him that night; he turned to and fro in misery, both of mind and body, unable to find rest. When the doctor arrived at last, the next morning, he told him plainly that he believed it was going to be a case of small-pox; and that he was a bad subject for it.

"But what am I to do?" cried Dick. "I'm all alone. There's nobody to give me bite or sup. What's to become of me?"

"I'll send you in a woman to attend to you," answered the doctor.

But though he lay listening all day for the welcome click of the latch of his unlocked door, and a woman's step in the room below, no such sound came to him. It was the doctor's step and voice he heard at last late on in the evening.

"There isn't a woman in the parish that will come near you," said the doctor, sternly; "they all say you've robbed your step-mother, and driven her and your brother into the workhouse; and they will not come near you."

"But will they let me die like a dog, with nobody to take care of me?" asked Dick, in an agony of terror.

"I won't say you'll die," answered the doctor, "but you'll be very ill, and death is not improbable. If I see you in great danger, I'll try if I can find somebody who knows nothing about you. But till then you must do the best you can. I or my assistant will see you twice a day; and there's no need to lock your door, for everybody knows you are down. I'll put food and water within your reach before I go away."

It was a terrible night to Dick Medlicott, and it was only the first of several nights and days of utter forsakenness. When he fell into a fitful and delirious sleep, he fancied he was already in eternity, where there were no longer hours and minutes, and the welcome change of day and night. So long it seemed, that when the grey dawn came at length, it almost terrified him, as if it was some new pain. The loud, shrill crowing of the cocks, and the chirping of the sparrows in the thatch, seemed, if possible, more intolerable than the death-like stillness of the dark; and as the noonday came, and the bright glare of the sun shone full upon him through the uncurtained window, he felt as if his torment was more than he could bear. And there was no one either in heaven or on earth that cared for him!

The doctor paid him a hurried visit in the morning, and his assistant came in the evening; but all the other hours were utterly lonely. He felt himself forsaken both by God and man. Then the recollection of his good old father came across him; and the remembrance of the first time he had entered this cottage, a boy of ten, welcomed and cared for by his step-mother, until his own bad conduct had banished him from this peaceful home. He thought of Gideon, too, who had always admired him with the tender admiration of a younger brother, and had been wont to follow him about like a faithful dog, overjoyed if he took the least kindly notice of him. If he had not been so great a fool, and so black a sinner, Gideon and his mother would have been beside him now.

In his delirious dreams he fancied he saw his father a long way off, sitting in a cool yet sunny spot, with Gideon, still a little child, folded in his arms; and both were happy, he could see that by their faces. And he called to them in his great misery, as he lay there tossing to and fro, and he could hear his own voice crying aloud, "Father, send Gideon, that he may dip the tip of his finger in water, and cool my tongue, for I am tormented in this flame." And his father's happy face grew sad, and he looked up to some one out of his sight, and said, "Lord, is it too late? Canst not Thou cross the great gulf, and save my poor son?" And a voice came down out of heaven, saying, "I know him not. Depart from me, all ye that work iniquity."

It was so awful to hear that sad, stern voice, that each time the terrible dream repeated itself he started up at the sound of it in a frenzy of dread, not knowing where to hide himself, or upon whom lie could call for help. For he knew there was no refuge, and none to deliver him from the wrath of God. If the Saviour Himself was against him, who then could be for him?

Nor was the horror of it lessened as the dream came over again and again. It grew more and more terrifying to him, until the first dreamy vision of the sunny spot where his father dwelt with Gideon in his arms, seemed to him a dreadful and appalling sight; and the sound of the voice of Him, whom he could not see, fell like a crash of thunder, full of tremendous threatenings, against him.

He was lying quite still, after a paroxysm of fear which left him utterly helpless, when suddenly in the room below him, which was all desolate and deserted, he heard the thin, aged voice of his dead father praying. He was awake now, wide awake; he knew where he was, and that the light shining into the room was the light of the moon. He was dangerously ill, yet there was no fellow-creature who would come near him. That he knew. But when he heard his father's voice in prayer on the old hearth below him, the fevered blood in his veins ran cold, and the bed shook beneath his trembling and aching frame. For he was not dreaming now; he was as wide awake as ever he had been in his life; yet quite clearly and distinctly could he hear what seemed his dead father's voice.

"Lord!" he was saying; "Thou has given Aby her heart's desire; the houses and the land are hers; Oh, give me mine, I pray thee, dear Lord. Didst Thou not hang on the accursed cross for my son Dick, as well as for every soul of man? Oh, my son, my son! Would God I could die for thee, my son, my son! Bring him home again, Lord, to Thee and me. Have mercy on him, O my God! have mercy on him, according to Thy loving kindness, according to the multitude of Thy tender mercies, blot out all his transgressions."

Then for a little while the voice was silent, and not a sound broke the dreadful stillness. But through the chinks in the floor he could see that there was a faint light in the room below. The clock struck one, as he lay scarcely daring to breathe. Then the prayer was uttered again, but in a lower tone, as of one exhausted by sore weeping and sobbing; and he heard the chair on the hearth pushed back, as though his father was rising from his knees. A footstep came slowly and quietly across the floor towards the steep staircase, and Dick could see that the light was burning. He started up with the strength of overpowering terror. His father's spirit was coming up the stairs to meet him face to face; and how could he bear to look upon it?

The light drew nearer, and grew brighter. The door, which had been left ajar by the doctor, was softly pushed wide open, and his straining eyes fell upon the mild and pleasant face of his brother Gideon.

Chapter VIII

Loving her Enemies

For some weeks after she had entered the Union Workhouse, and was clothed in pauper dress and ate pauper food, Abigail had been like one crushed by the vastness of the calamity that had befallen her and Gideon. During all her busy life the faintest dread of such a trouble had never crossed her mind. Even if she failed to buy back the houses, every pound she added to her father's store which he had left to her, made the prospect of her old age more comfortable. But she had bought them back; and no law could make it just for her step-son to rob her of them. There were not many persons she could tell her tale to, and none of them could help her. The chaplain of the workhouse told her there was no redress.

"Couldn't her Majesty, the Queen, help me, if she knew?" asked Abigail, in her extremity of despair; "I've prayed for her every Sunday morning in church, and Richard prayed for her often of an evening. Couldn't she see justice done me?"

"The Queen might take you out of the workhouse, and provide for you in other ways, but she could not give you back the houses," was the answer.

But it was the old place itself Abigail was homesick for. If she could not return, and end her days under the roof which had sheltered her all her life, it mattered little to her where she spent her last few years. In her trouble the old Bible so well thumbed by her husband, occupied much of her time; and how new and fresh the words seemed to her! For whilst the world deals well with us, and life is busy and prosperous, the familiar verses sound like an old song to us, falling on our ears unheard; but when sorrow and loneliness come to dwell with us, then they are as a voice from heaven, telling us of our Father there, and the Lord who has passed through life and death before us.

Abigail's greatest fear was lest Gideon should be ill-treated by the men, in whose ward he had to live. But the workhouse matron quickly discovered how useful the willing half-witted lad could be to her, and she kept him almost constantly employed in the kitchen, and in going on errands for her. Scarcely a day passed in which he did not see his mother; and when the wintry weather was fine enough, she could shelter herself in a sunny corner of the women's yard, where only a high wall separated it from the old men's court, and there listen if she could but catch the sound of Gideon's voice, singing some of the old hymns they had often sung together at home.

And when the rain or snow kept her a prisoner in the bare, comfortless ward, where a crowd of shivering old women wrangled over the warmest seats near the fire, Abigail learned to sit still, and patiently brood over the life of our Lord and Saviour. She could read but slowly; but as she read she forgot her pain, and sorrow, and loneliness. The whitewashed walls, the long row of beds, the grey sky peering in through the high windows, all were forgotten as she read for herself the verses she had been used to hear from her husband's lips, hardly knowing whether they were his words, or the Lord's.

So the long idle winter crept gradually away, and Easter was coming again. She was keeping in her heart the anniversary of her husband's death, and going over again the happy years she had lived with him in the old home she would see no more, when late one evening the matron entered the ward, and came up to her bed where she was quietly sitting on the chair beside it, doing nothing but ponder sadly yet patiently on the change that had come to her life and Gideon's.

"Aby," she said, "here's the doctor come from your old place, and he says your step-son, Dick Medlicott's dying of small-pox, and he can't get a nurse for him for love nor money. He's driven over on purpose to ask if there's any of the men willing to go to him, but not one of them'll stir, except poor Gideon, and he's wild to be off to his brother Dick. But he doesn't know what the danger is, poor fellow; and we couldn't let him go without your consent."

"Dyin' o' small-pox!" repeated Abigail, in a scared tone.

"Ay! there's a bare chance for him, the doctor says," answered the matron, "if he can only find a nurse for him. But he lies there all day in a high fever, and nobody to give him so much as a drop of water. And if he begins to ramble he might get out o' doors, and die in the fields, or do himself a mischief."

"I'll go," cried Abigail, rising quickly.

"No, no; not you," she continued. "It wants a strong man to hold him in bed, and keep him out o' mischief when he's raving. Gideon could do it, but not you; and Gideon's crying to be off. But he hasn't sense enough to see his danger; and the doctor told me to ask you."

"No; I canna run the risk o' losin' Gideon!" cried Abigail, in terror.

"And I'm not the one to blame you," said the matron, "it'll be a rare good thing for you, if Dick does die; the houses'll come to Gideon by rights. Let him die and go to his own place, I say."

She turned away, and Abigail's eyes followed her as she paced briskly down the long ward. Only this morning she had been dwelling upon the Lord's words, so often spoken by her husband: "I say unto you, Love your enemies, bless them that curse you, do good to them that hate you, and pray for them which despitefully use you and persecute you; that ye may be the children of your Father which is in heaven." They had seemed hard words to her, but she had so far obeyed them as to pray for Dick and his friend Jenkins. But now she was suddenly called upon to do what was far harder than praying for her step-son. He was dying of a loathsome and dangerous disease, abandoned by all his fellow-creatures, and the poor simple Gideon alone was willing to watch beside him. They would not let him go without her consent; but how could she bring herself to consent?

Yet just as the door closed upon the matron, Aby sprang from her seat, and ran after her almost as if she was once more young and active. She followed her across the dusky yard, and into the outer court where the doctor's gig was standing and Gideon holding the horse's head. She threw her arms about him, and pressed him closely to her heart. He was all she had in the world now; yet she could not disobey her Lord by keeping him out of the danger he was about to meet. But she must run the same risk too.

"Let us both go," she said, eagerly; "Gideon and me. I can take care of 'em both. If Gideon dies, may be the Lord'll let me die too. I canna let Gideon go alone."

"Aby," answered the doctor kindly, patting her shoulder; "my gig won't hold you both to-night; and Dick is in sore need of some one to tend him at once. Gideon can do all that's wanted through the night; and

I'll send for you to-morrow. I'll set him down at the turn where the Watling Street runs up into the road, and he'll find his way home safe enough, won't you, my lad?"

"Father's home where Dick is," said Gideon; "ay, poor Dick, he'll be glad to see me at home again, won't he, mother? May be father'll be there too, the Lord Jesus'll let him go home for a bit, if he's wanted, I'm sure. I'd like to see father again, now, and Dick."

"I shall ha' to let thee go," said Abigail, weeping; "but I'll start off first thing in the mornin' to come to thee. The Lord take care of thee for me, and watch over thee till I see thy face again."

"Ay! ay! mother," he answered cheerily, climbing up into the doctor's gig, his face radiant with delight. Abigail watched them as they drove down the short and narrow street, and then turned back to the cold workhouse ward, and crept quietly to bed, praying there through the long hours of the night that no harm might befall Gideon.

Chapter IX

Depths of Mercy

Abigail could not wait the next day for the doctor's gig, but set off as soon as she could get out on her walk homewards. It did not weary her as the tramp out to the workhouse had done; and as she caught sight of the old thatched roof and gable windows of her house, the tears blinded her, and her heart beat fast. She was an aged, worn-out woman, in the workhouse dress, crossing her father's door-sill as a pauper. But it was her fathers house, and her boy Gideon was there, a pauper like herself, but altogether unconscious of any shame. Why should she be ashamed? Jesus had endured the cross, despising the shame, and had entered into His father's house with the print of the nails on His hands, and may be among His many crowns He still wore His crown of thorns. She hurried on along the old garden path, bordered now with more weeds than flowers, and opened the old door.

Ah! how different the house was since she had left it, nearly a year ago! Then the oak dresser opposite the window shone till she could almost see her face in it, and the pewter plates on the shelves above it glittered like silver. Now, everything was dingy and dirty, a shock and grief to her. The ashes on the hearth were heaped up into a dusty pile, on which a handful of embers were burning, and her own little kettle, once as bright as the pewter plates, hung over them as black as a coal. But she had no time to linger there, though her hands tingled to set to work. She must go on upstairs.

And now, at this moment, Gideon's voice caught her ear, singing in a low, soft tone, as if he was lulling a pining child to sleep; and the words he sang were those of a favourite hymn of her husband's:—

"Depth of mercy, can there be
Mercy still reserved for me?
Can my God His wrath forbear?
Me, the chief of sinners, spare?

She stood on the stairs listening to his lowered voice, until suddenly he sang, loudly and clearly, as if some blessed vision were revealed to him:—

There for me the Saviour stands,
Shows His wounds, and spreads His hands!
God is love! I know, I feel;
Jesus weeps, and loves me still"

"Is it true?" asked Dick's husky and troubled voice; "does Jesus spread His hands to me, as well as to thee?"

Gideon went on singing joyously:—
"Jesus, answer from above,
Is not all Thy nature love?
Wilt thou not the wrong forget?
Suffer me to kiss Thy feet."

"Oh! if the Lord 'ud only let me crawl to his feet!" cried Dick; "oh! if He could forgive me If mother and thee could forgive me! But thou knows nothin' o' sin, my poor Gideon. If some fellow-sinner could come, and tell me as Jesus'll forgive me, may be I could believe it. But thou'rt a peer innocent, as simple as a child."

"I'm here, Dick," said Abigail, pushing open the door, and stepping into the room.

The coarse border of the workhouse cap fitting closely round her grey and sunken face, so changed from its sunburnt, healthy look, and the dark blue print gown, and check handkerchief pinned across her breast, showed plainly enough what place she had come from. Dick turned his swollen and discoloured face towards her, and gazed at her through his half-blinded eyes, a pitiable creature, who stirred her heart to its very depths.

"It's me, Dick, thy mother, my poor boy," she hastened to say; "I'd ha' come before if I'd known, and I let Gideon come last night, when the doctor wanted help. I've forgiven thee, Dick, in my very heart, God knows. It's been a hard thing to do, for the houses were my father's before me, and he'd ha' turned in his grave if he'd known of it; but I've done it, my poor, poor Dick."

"Mother!" cried Dick, raising himself up in bed, and stretching out his arms to her. He had felt himself forsaken, abandoned by God and man; and here was Gideon, and his mother had come to him too! She drew near to him, and stooped down that he might put his arms round her neck, while she clasped hers about him, he was a penitent sinner at last; and there was joy over him in heaven, where Richard was. She laid him down on the pillow again, where his father's dying head had lain, and smoothed the bed-clothes about him.

"Canst thee forgive me?" he gasped, as he lay panting for breath, and looking up beseechingly into her face.

"Didn't I say as I'd forgiven thee?" she asked, ay! like Jesus forgives us afore we ask Him. hadn't He forgiven us when He died on the cross for us? Eh! if I hadna forgiven thee I could niver ha' sent my boy Gideon to nurse thee through the small-pox. If thy dear father was here, he'd tell thee as God is waitin' to forgive us, stretchin' out his arms all the day long, and callin', callin', to come back and get our sins pardoned, and our hearts made new. Thy father 'ud tell thee to think of that verse, 'Come and let us reason together, saith the Lord; though your sins be as scarlet, they shall be white as snow; though they be red like crimson, they shall be as wool.' I've heard him say that hundreds and hundreds o' times; and thee has heard him too, my poor lad."

"It's too late," he murmured; "I canna make thee any amends."

"No; we canna make amends," she answered; "but Him as died for us'll do that. He's made it up to me for bein' in the workhouse; He's been so near to me, and so precious. The hymn says, 'Jesus weeps, and loves us still!' 'Eh! lad, He loves thee; ay! and I love thee, spite of all. Should I be here, Dick, if I hated thee, and cursed thee, and wished thee harm?"

"No," he whispered.

"And it's a poor thing to liken me to Him," she went on; "but would Jesus ha' hung upon the cross, if He'd hated us sinners, and wished us harm? Would He ha' cried out to God, as He was a-dyin', 'Father, forgive them; they know not what they do?' None on us know what we're a-doin' when we give way to sin. Thou didn't know as thou'd drive us into the workhouse, and fall into this misery thyself. If thou'd only been a good man, like thy father, none o' these things 'ud ha' come to pass."

"No, no!" he answered, turning painfully on his bed, and shutting his swollen eyelids.

"And now thou be quiet," she said soothingly; "and Gideon, as soon as he's had his breakfast, 'ill come and sit beside thee. We'll not quit thee again while thou'rt ill, my poor Dick." He listened to her gentle movements in the room below, which had seemed empty and dreary until now; and oh! What an inexpressible comfort to him it was. Strange fancies still flitted across his delirious brain at times; but they were no longer terrifying. Again he saw his father and Gideon sitting in safety in a cool yet sunny spot; and their faces shone with gladness; but when he called aloud to him, and said "Father," instead of asking him for a drop of water to cool his parched tongue, he cried, "I have sinned against heaven, and before thee, and am no more worthy to be called thy son." And then he heard the voice of One whom he could not even yet see, and it seemed to say gladly, "This my son was dead, and is alive again; he was lost, and is found." And whenever Dick came to himself after this dream, he found the tears were rolling down his face, and a strange sense of mingled sorrow and peace filled his soul.

But the turning-point of his disease was not yet come. Before the next morning Dick's life was despaired of, and only a slender thread of hope linked it to this world. Abigail watched beside him as she had watched by his father and her own father, in this old home of hers. Very full of perplexing thoughts was her troubled mind. Was Dick's repentance true? Would he, if he lived, lead henceforth a Christian life, like his father's? If that were so, how happily and peacefully she could spend the remainder of her days, and leave Gideon at last under his brother's care. Not if it was only the terror of approaching death, and the dread of meeting God as his Judge, which had wrought this change in him; as soon as he recovered he would quickly turn aside again to his evil ways, and she must go back to the workhouse to die there, and leave Gideon to the chances and changes of a very cold and cruel world.

But if Dick died? Yes; then the old place would be Gideon's; so lawyer Whitmore told her. All would be right for him as long as she lived; but what would become of him afterwards? God only knew.

"Mother!" said Dick's faint voice, calling to her in calm, collected tones, and she stooped over him to listen; "I pray Jesus to forgive me, and if I live I'll make thee amends for all I've done. Hast thee asked God to let me live?"

"Ay! I have Dick, He knows," she answered; "if Gideon and me have to go back to the workhouse for it."

"I'd never ha' done it but for the law," he murmured; "but if I live, I'll see if the law can be broke somehow. I'd rather die than live and be wicked again. Kiss me, mother."

She knelt down beside him, and stretched her arm across him, as she had done across his dying father, and kissed his poor swollen lips as tenderly as if they had been the sweet fresh mouth of a little child. When she moved again his eyelids were closed, and his breathing came soft and regular as that of a sleeping child.

It was some weeks before Dick Medlicott was well enough to venture far from home; but the first visit he made was to the village lawyer to get his stepmother's cottages legally settled upon herself, with the power to will them as she pleased. He wished for as little delay as possible in doing this, for every one except Jenkins would be rejoiced to see Abigail have her own again. Dick had not told her what he was about to do, and her heart was somewhat troubled as she watched him go down Watling Street towards the village leaning on Gideon's strong arm. If he was going to the "Barley Mow" all her new-born hopes would perish miserably.

"Mother," he said, after he had returned, tired out with the short journey; "I wish thee'd invite the old meeting to come back to the old place. If they'll have me I'm going to join in with them, and try to be something like father. Anyhow ask 'em to come here next Wednesday."

It was a glad day for Abigail when the old neighbours assembled once more in her pleasant kitchen. Richard was not there to lead them; but she did not doubt that he knew Dick was there, the prodigal son come home at last. When his turn came to speak of God's dealings with him, he could not sit still, but stood up, leaning his hand on the back of his chair.

"I'm a wicked sinner," he said; "but Jesus Christ has pardoned me; and to show I'm true and I'm not makin' any pretence, I've been to lawyer Whitmore and found out the way of makin' over the houses to mother, as they rightfully belong to. And I beg her pardon here, before you all, and I ask her to let me try to be a good son to her, and a good brother to poor Gideon."

His voice trembled, and when he ended a dead silence followed. A stronger feeling ran through the little assembly, than when Abigail had triumphantly praised God for giving her her heart's desire. The recovery of a lost soul to the fold of Christ was a greater marvel, and a far greater blessing. Tears stood in the eyes of the grave, placid countrymen and women; and Abigail's sobs at last broke the stillness. Than they pressed round Dick, shaking hands with him, and bidding him welcome among them.

Her old age was almost happier to Abigail than her married life had been. Dick, who had learned his father's trade as a boy, took it up again as his means of livelihood, and settled down in her house as if he had been indeed her own son. He and Gideon made her life easy for her; Gideon obeying his elder brother's will with simple fidelity. As the years went by, proving Dick's repentance a true one, and himself a changed man, all her fears for her boy's future, after she was gone, were altogether removed. The old roof would cover her and him until they were both called up higher into their Father's house.

SARAH SMITH (writing as Hesba Stretton) – A CONCISE BIBLIOGRAPHY

Short Stories & Periodicals
The Lucky Leg (19th March 1859)
The Ghost in the Clock Room (Christmas, 1859)
The Postmaster's Daughter (All the Year Round, 5th November 1859)
A Provincial Post Office (All the Year Round, 28 February 1863)
Jessica's First Prayer (Sunday at Home, July 1866)
The Travelling Post-Office (All the Year Round, Mugby Junction, December 1866)
Jessica's Mother (1867)

Books
Fern's Hollow (1864)
Enoch Roden's Training (1865)
The Children of Cloverley (1865)
Jessica's First Prayer (Sunday at Home, July 1866)
The Fishers of Derby Haven (1866)
Jessica's Mother (Periodical 1867, book 1904)
Pilgrim Street (1867)
Little Meg's Children (1868)
Alone in London (1869)
Nellie's Dark Days (1870)
The Doctor's Dilemma (1872)
The King's Servants (1873)
Lost Gip (1873
Cassy (1874)
Brought Home (1875)
In Prison and Out (1878)
Two Secrets (1882)
The Lord's Purse-Bearers (1883)
Sam Franklin's Savings Bank (1888)
Little Meg's Children (1905)
The Christmas Child (1909 in US)

Other Works
Brought Home
Cobwebs And Cables

www.ingramcontent.com/pod-product-compliance
Lightning Source LLC
Chambersburg PA
CBHW061506170626
46811CB00004B/1631